Tracy
Halverson

A ... Danger

by

Jane McManus

Watermill Press

Printed in the United States of America

Illustrations by Thomas Heggie

ISBN 0-89375-802-7

Contents

The Dummies That Saved the Day

Rose was waiting in the women's lounge on the third floor of Green's Department Store. Her eyes were heavy. She looked at her watch. It was 8:15 P.M. *Anne is always late,* Rose thought. *She'd better get here soon. We won't have time to get Ms. Brown's present.*

Rose pulled her legs up on the sofa. *I'll just close my eyes for a minute*, she thought. She rested her head against the sofa. In a few minutes, Rose was sound asleep.

Rose woke up two hours later. It was dark. "What happened?" she said in an alarmed voice. "Did someone just shut off the light?" There was no answer.

Rose stood up and felt her way along the wall. She stumbled over a table as she tried to find the door. When she opened the door, she expected to see a bright store full of last-minute shoppers. But the only lights she saw were the exit lights at the stairways. The rest of the store was dark. There were no people to be seen.

I don't like this, Rose said to herself. *Where is everyone? Where is Anne?* She started to walk toward one of the exit signs. "Ouch!" she exclaimed as she bumped into a counter. The store seemed to be full of strange shapes and dark objects. Nothing looked familiar anymore.

I've got to get out of here, she thought. As she groped along, she suddenly felt a hand on her shoulder. "Help!" she screamed and whipped around. She threw out her arm to ward off the hand and knocked over a display manikin. It clattered to the ground. Then there was silence again.

Rose's heart pounded. Her knees trembled so much that she found it hard to walk. *It's only a dummy!* she said to herself. *This is crazy! I shouldn't be so frightened by the dark.*

Rose moved forward slowly again. She reached out as if she were a blind person exploring a new room. Inching her way along, she finally reached the stairway exit.

Maybe there are lights on the second floor, she thought. She reached for the stair railing and held it tightly. Then she carefully went down the stairs.

The second floor was as dark as the third. Rose held her watch up close to the light from the second-floor exit sign. It was 10:45. "That's why it's dark in here!" Rose exclaimed. "The store is closed. I guess I shut my eyes for more than a few minutes."

What a spot to be in! she thought. *How can I get out without setting off a burglar alarm?*

Just then, she saw a beam of light from the other side of the store. A man with a flashlight came in a side exit door. "Hey!" Rose called.

It must be a security guard, she thought. *He'll help me.*

*A man with a flashlight came in a
side exit door.*

Then the light went out. No one answered her, but she could hear things being knocked over. Someone was coming in her direction. *Why doesn't the guard turn the flashlight back on?* she thought. *Why didn't he answer me?*

Suddenly, Rose knew what was happening. *That's not a security guard,* she thought. *That's a burglar! And he knows I saw him. He's coming to get me!*

She turned and grabbed for the stair railing. She stumbled, hurrying down the stairs to the first floor. *I've got to get out of here even if I do set off the burglar alarm,* she thought. She tried to open the outside door at the foot of the stairs. It was locked. She pulled and pulled.

Then she heard noise at the top of the stairs. She ran into the shopping area on the first floor. *Maybe the front doors will open,* she thought. She raced toward the front of the store. But she couldn't get those doors open, either.

I have to hide, she thought. She looked around in panic. Then she heard noise near the foot of the stairs. *He's coming! I can't escape!*

Suddenly, Rose thought of the display window beside the front door. She pulled back the curtain. She stepped up into the window with the manikins. Traffic sped by in the street. Rose waved at the passing cars. One woman waved back.

Oh no, Rose thought. *Things like this are only supposed to happen on television.* She heard footsteps coming closer. *I'm trapped!* she thought. *There's nowhere else to run.*

Rose was frozen with fear. She heard

*Rose stepped up into the window
with the manikins.*

the footsteps by the front door. She saw a hand pull back the curtain to the display windows. But she still couldn't move. The man stood there and looked right at her — and then right past her. He closed the curtain and walked away.

Rose thought she would faint. She grabbed one of the manikins for support. *He thought I was a dummy,* she realized. Her heart was beating so fast she felt as if it were going to explode.

Just then, a police car pulled up in front of the store. Anne and a police officer got out. They looked around. Rose frantically waved her arms.

When they saw her in the window, their eyes opened wide. She shaped the word "Help!" with her mouth. They nodded. Then she shaped the words, "Someone is in the store." She pointed behind her.

The officer ran to the police car to use

13

the radio. Within minutes, two more police cars were outside the store. A man in a business suit got out of one of the cars. He opened the store. Three officers followed him inside.

Rose quickly told everyone what had happened. She described the man she had seen. Then she and Anne were taken to a small office for safety.

Soon, the store was filled with light. The officers found the man hiding in a dressing room. They put him under guard in one of the police cars.

"He's an escaped prisoner," said the officer who came with Anne. "He broke into the store to steal clothes and money."

"You're lucky he didn't find you," Anne said.

"He did find me," Rose answered. "But he thought I was a dummy."

"Oh, you're no dummy," Anne replied

with a laugh. "I'm the dummy. This wouldn't have happened if I hadn't forgotten where to meet you."

"That was pretty dumb," Rose said. "But I fell asleep in the lounge. That's not so bright either."

"For dummies, you two saved the day! That's not bad," said the officer, smiling. "But I'm taking you home now. Tomorrow morning, come to the police station. You need to make a full report. Be there at nine."

"If I can remember where to go," Anne said.

"And if I wake up in time,"Rose added with a laugh.

It's Not Hunting Season

Tess skied away from the farmhouse. Yesterday, she had made a path to the barn. During the night, the snow had covered it. Everything was heaped with soft, white flakes.

Tess glided past the barn. It made her feel good to think of the animals safe and warm inside.

She looked up into the swirling snowflakes. "What a wonderful day!" she said. There was no one around to hear her, but that didn't matter.

Tess skied across the corn field. She went into the woods. Everything was very quiet. The evergreens were covered with snow. Bushes looked like little hills of cotton.

As Tess skied on, she saw some deer tracks. *It would be great to see a deer,* she thought. She skied along the ridge of a hill.

Soon, she caught sight of the deer tracks again. Turning smoothly on her skis, she decided to follow the tracks.

Tess skied deeper into the woods. Suddenly, the tracks turned sharply to the left and disappeared under some bushes.

Tess skied to a stop. *I've lost the deer,*

she thought sadly. But around the other side of the bushes, the deer tracks continued. There was another set of tracks, too.

It's a fawn, Tess thought with a smile. She could tell by the size of the new tracks. She peered into the forest ahead of her. Then she caught her breath in surprise. Tess could see the two deer only a few yards away.

Just then, the sound of a rifle shot echoed through the woods. Birds flew out of the bushes. Tess dropped to her knees and looked around. She couldn't see anyone.

It's not hunting season, she thought. *But that definitely was a rifle shot.*

Tess looked up from where she crouched in the snow. Moments before, two deer had been standing. Now, there was only one — the fawn. The big deer was lying on the ground. She was wounded, but still moving.

Tess skied slowly toward the animals. She spoke softly so they wouldn't be frightened.

"I'll get help for you," she told the deer. "I know you don't understand me, but don't worry. I'll be back with help. I'll bring food for your fawn, too."

Tess looked around to get her bearings. Then she raced off through the woods towards the farm. Soon, she heard sounds behind her. Suddenly, a bullet slammed into the tree in front of her.

That hunter must think I'm a deer! she thought. She screamed as loudly as she could, "Stop, you fool!"

He's getting close enough to kill me, Tess realized. She started to ski very fast. Then she remembered the ravine. It was a deep, narrow ditch just ahead. She couldn't go as quickly as she wanted

"I'll get help for you," Tess told the deer.

to there. She might fall in. And the snow made it too hard to tell where the edges of the ravine were.

Soon, she was on safe ground again, heading down a hill. Her skis whirred through the snow. She was grateful for the skis. They made it possible for her to move more quickly than the hunter.

Just half a mile more, she thought, *and I'll be at the farm.* Then she heard a crash and a terrible scream of pain.

Tess stopped in her tracks and listened. The scream continued. *That awful hunter must have fallen into the ravine,* she thought. For a second, she was glad. *It serves him right,* she thought. *He left the doe and the fawn to die. He probably didn't tell anyone he was going hunting out of season. If I don't say anything, he'll be in real trouble.*

Tess listened to the pain in the

hunter's voice as he cried for help. *I have to help him,* she said to herself as she turned in his direction. *I could never come in these woods again if I didn't help him.*

Tess skied back carefully along the top of the ravine. She looked for the hunter's tracks in the snow. She followed the sound of his cries.

Soon she saw him. He was lying on his back in the ravine. His left leg was twisted beneath him. His rifle was in the snow five feet away.

When the hunter saw Tess, he cried out, "My leg is broken! Help me! You've got to help me!"

Tess looked down at him. Then she called, "You wounded a doe and left her to die. Why should I help you?"

"But I didn't know," he cried.

"You should have found out," Tess

*Tess skied back carefully along the edge
of the ravine.*

answered. "You almost killed me, too. You're not even supposed to be hunting now. I'm not going to help you. Just lie there and freeze like the doe." She turned and skied out of his sight.

"No! No!" he cried out. "Come back! Help me! I'll never do it again!"

Tess skied back to the edge of the ravine. "Is that a promise?" she asked.

"Yes," he cried. "Yes, I promise."

"O.K.," Tess answered. "I'm going for help—for you and the deer." She turned and skied as fast as she could for the farm.

In less than an hour, the rescue squad arrived. They took the hunter out of the woods. He was still in pain. But he was grateful.

Tess watched him go by on the stretcher. She was glad she had helped him, even though he had almost killed her.

Then Tess led her parents to the doe. She was still alive. The fawn was still there, too. Tess spoke softly to the fawn. She held out food. Slowly it came to her. As it reached for the food, Tess slipped a rope around its neck.

"You'll be safe now, little animal," she said.

Her parents put the doe on a sled. They all started back through the snow-filled woods to the farm.

Tess looked up into the snowy sky. She looked at the animals and her parents. "This has been the most exciting day I've ever had!" she said.

The Perfect Place for a Murder

Jean's desk was covered with paper. She had been writing all day.

"That's it!" she exclaimed. She put down her pen.

"What's it?" her niece, Tess, asked. Tess had just arrived to have dinner with her aunt.

"The perfect place for a murder!" Jean answered. "I've just worked out the perfect place to commit a murder."

"You should be more careful, Aunt Jean," Tess warned. "Someone might hear you." Tess looked over her shoulder.

"Nonsense, dear," Jean answered. "I don't commit murders. I just make up stories about people who do."

Jean got up from her desk. "Let's go out to dinner tonight, Tess," she said. "I was writing well this afternoon. I didn't want to stop and cook."

"O.K.," Tess said. "But promise me you won't talk in public about committing murder."

Jean laughed and put her arm around Tess's shoulders. They walked to the door.

"We'll go to the new restaurant on the waterfront," Jean said.

At dinner, they talked about everything but murder. They had a wonderful time.

"You've been very good, Aunt Jean," Tess smiled. "You haven't said a word about crime since we got here."

"I've been saving it up until after dinner," Jean answered. "I want to show you the perfect place to commit a 'you-know-what.'" Jean looked over her shoulder, pretending she didn't want anyone to hear her.

"Oh, Aunt Jean," Tess laughed. "It's a good thing you're my favorite aunt, or you'd drive me crazy."

"Come on," Jean said. She led her niece from the restaurant. "It's not too far from here."

"I don't want to get anywhere near the

"Come on," Jean said. "It's not too far from here."

perfect place for a murder," Tess answered.

"Oh, don't worry," Jean said. "I've got it all figured out for my novel." She started walking along the beach. "Pretend the restaurant isn't here," Jean said. "It won't be in my novel. Imagine this — it's a cloudy, dark night. The beach is empty."

"I don't need to imagine that," Tess answered. "It *is* dark and cloudy. Around the bend is the most deserted part of the waterfront." Tess shivered. "I don't like it here at all," she said. "Let's go back. You can check it out it in the daytime." She stopped walking.

"I need to look at it at night," Jean answered. "I need to see what kind of shadows that abandoned pier makes." Her eyes sparkled with excitement.

"Come on," Jean said. "Just a little bit

farther. There's nothing to be frightened of."

Tess walked on slowly. "All right," she said, "but I'm not going past those rocks."

"Look," Jean whispered, "we can't even see the restaurant. We're all alone here."

"Why are you whispering?" Tess asked. She was getting more nervous with every step.

"It's more exciting that way," Jean answered. "Do you see that old pier ahead? That's where my murder is going to take place. It's so perfect. I don't know why no one has thought of it yet."

"Maybe someone has," Tess whispered. She stopped suddenly. "I thought I just saw something move out there." Her face got very white. "I don't want to go any farther," she said. "I don't think you should either."

Jean stopped, too. "Dear," she said, "you look so pale. Come over here and sit down." She led her niece to a big pile of rocks.

"Now, dear," Jean said, trying to calm her niece.

"Look!" Tess interrupted. She pointed toward the old pier. "I knew someone was there." She pulled her aunt down behind the rocks.

"My goodness!" Jean whispered. "You're right! There are two men!"

"They're coming this way," Tess said. "It's too late to run. They'd see us."

"We'll hide here until they're gone," Jean answered. "They're probably just out for a walk."

As the two men got closer, Jean and Tess could hear them talking.

"You were right, Sam," one of the men

said. "This *is* the perfect place for a murder!"

"Yeah," said Sam. "If she comes to, she won't be able to get that rope untangled before the tide comes in."

"When they find her, it will look as if she got tangled up while she was swimming, and drowned."

Sam laughed. "Not bad! Not bad at all!" He slapped the other man on the back.

"When you hire Eddie Blake to bump someone off, you get service," the man said proudly.

Soon, the two men had passed the pile of rocks where Tess and Jean were hiding. They continued walking along the beach.

"It sounds as if they're talking about a real murder!" Tess whispered. Her eyes were open very wide. "We should get the

"When you hire Eddie Blake to bump someone off, you get service," the man said.

police! This is not a story. This is real."

"We don't have time to get the police," Jean answered. "We've got to find the body before the tide comes in."

Jean jumped to her feet. She looked around to see if she could see anyone. The men were out of sight. She started to run toward the pier. Tess raced after her.

"I bet they left the body under the pier," Jean said. "That's what I was going to do in my novel. There are old mooring ropes there."

Soon they were crawling around under the old pier. "There's something over there," Tess called softly. They moved toward a dark shape in the sand.

"It's a woman," Tess gasped. "She's all tangled in the rope that's tied to the pier. She's alive, though. I can see her breathing."

"We have to get her loose," Jean said.

"The tide has already started to come in," said Tess. "We don't have much time to untangle all this rope."

"I've got a jackknife," Jean said. She started to cut through the ropes. Tess tried to untangle what she could. The dark ocean water was getting closer every minute.

"Hurry, Aunt Jean," Tess cried. "The tide is almost at her feet."

"It's so hard to see," said Jean. "I don't want to cut her."

"But if we don't get her loose, she'll drown," Tess said.

"You're right," Jean answered. She cut through the ropes more fiercely. Soon, she had all but one big rope cut. But by now, the water was up around the woman's waist.

"Keep going, Aunt Jean, keep going!"

Tess urged her aunt. "I'll hold her head up out of the water!" Tess lifted the woman's head.

Just as the water reached the woman's chin, Jean cried out, "She's free!"

Tess and Jean pulled her quickly through the water to the beach.

"Murder is *awful!*" Tess cried when they were on dry land at last.

"Yes, it is," Jean answered. "But she's still alive. And I can't see any blood. I don't think I cut her."

"Now we've got to get her to the hospital," Tess said.

"And we've got to get the police after those men," Jean answered.

"You can write about all this in your novel," Tess said.

"I don't think so," Jean said after a moment. "It's too close for comfort. I'm

*Just as the water reached the woman's chin,
Jean cried out, "She's free!"*

going to have to find another perfect place for a murder."

Tess looked at her aunt in amazement.

"Don't worry," Jean said. "I'll check it out, but *only* in the daytime."

The Bad Dream

Julie moved restlessly in her sleep. "We're going to crash!" she screamed. "The plane is going to crash!"

She sat up in bed. Her eyes snapped open. *Oh, no,* she thought. *I did it again.*

Just then, the bedroom door opened. Mrs. Novak hurried over to the bed.

Oh, no, *Julie thought.* I
did it again.

"Julie, wake up," she said. "You're having that bad dream again."

"I'm all right," Julie said. "I'm sorry I woke you." Julie was embarrassed. She had disturbed everyone for the second night in a row.

"Your parents are going to be upset with me when they get home," Mrs. Novak said. "I should never have taken you to that movie about the plane crash."

"My parents won't be mad," Julie said. "They were glad I could stay with you while they went away. Besides, I'm not going to dream about plane crashes anymore. I'm really not."

"That's good," Mrs. Novak said. "Now try to get back to sleep."

The next morning, Julie went back to her own house to take care of her dog Scamp. She took him for a long walk in a field by some woods. Scamp ran on ahead of her, scaring grasshoppers and chasing butterflies. Julie watched Scamp play.

I wish Mom and Dad weren't flying home, she thought.

Suddenly, Julie heard the sound of an airplane in the distance. She turned and looked up to the sky. There was a small plane flying very low over the tops of the trees. It seemed to be heading toward the field. Smoke trailed from both engines.

"That plane's going to crash!" Julie cried out.

Just then, the sound of the motor stopped, and the plane disappeared into the trees. Julie heard a crash. Then there was not another sound. Julie rubbed her eyes. She couldn't see any sign of the plane crash.

She raced back toward the Novaks'

house. Scamp chased after her. Julie was out of breath when she ran in the back door.

"There's been a plane crash!" Julie cried. "In the woods!"

"I thought you weren't going to dream about plane crashes anymore," Mrs. Novak said.

"This isn't a dream!" Julie exclaimed. "It happened!"

"I don't think that's funny," Mrs. Novak said angrily. "Bring Scamp back home. We're going to pick up your parents."

Julie ran outside with tears streaming down her face. "She thinks I'm just imagining things!" Julie cried. She ran back toward the field. Scamp knew something was wrong. He ran right beside her.

When Julie got to the field, she looked

at where she had last seen the plane. There was still no sign that anything had happened. *I know there was a plane crash*, she said to herself. *I know there was. I'm not having a bad dream now.*

"What should I do?" she asked Scamp. He looked up at her and tilted his head to one side. "If I don't go back to the Novaks', everybody will be upset. I'll miss Mom and Dad at the airport."

But what if somebody's hurt in there? Julie asked herself. Then she started to run toward the woods. Scamp raced after her.

The woods were very thick. Julie felt the words "plane crash, plane crash" pound in her head as her sneakers hit the ground.

Strange shadows seemed to move in the woods. Julie wished she were on her way to the airport to get her parents.

She wished she were anywhere but running through these woods. She didn't want to find somebody who was badly hurt — or maybe even dead.

Julie had run past the area where she expected to find the plane. *Maybe it* was *a bad dream*, she thought. She stopped and looked all around her. "Maybe I just imagined it," she said to Scamp. "Maybe I'm going crazy." Tears started to fill her eyes again.

Suddenly, she heard a moan. She held her breath and listened. "There it is again!" she cried. Scamp started to bark. "Find him, Scamp!" Julie yelled.

Scamp bounded off over the top of a little hill. Julie raced after him. On the other side of the hill was the plane. Both wings had been ripped off in the crash. The body of the plane was slightly twisted but all in one piece.

The pilot lay slumped over the edge of the cockpit. There was a big gash on his forehead, and blood had dried on his cheek. He moved his head a little. He opened his eyes and looked at Julie. "Plane crash . . . bad dream," he mumbled.

"No, it wasn't a dream," Julie said. "There really was a crash. It's going to be all right now, though."

The pilot tried to lift his head and then passed out again.

Julie told Scamp, "Stay." He sat down by the plane. Then Julie dashed back through the woods. She followed the sun, heading straight to the field. Just as she came out of the woods, she saw her parents hurrying across the field.

Julie started to run even faster. Her parents ran, too, when they saw her. Soon they were in each other's arms.

"A plane crash!" Julie cried.

47

Julie started to run even faster.

"Yes," her father said. "We knew there must have been one when Mrs. Novak told us why you didn't come to pick us up. A rescue squad from the airport is on its way. They'll find the plane."

"I found it!" Julie exclaimed. "The pilot is hurt. I was just going for help. I'll lead you back to the plane. Scamp's guarding it."

Julie and her father ran back toward the wreck. When they got near, Scamp started to bark. But he stayed right beside the plane.

"Good dog, Scamp," Julie said. She ran over and patted him on the head. Then she and her father lifted the pilot carefully out of the plane. When they laid him on the ground, he opened his eyes.

"You came back," he said when he saw Julie. "It's not a bad dream."

"The rescue squad will be here very soon," she said. "Don't worry. You're going to be O.K."

"Thanks to you," he said and closed his eyes.

"That's right, Julie," her father said. "Thanks to you."

The Watcher

It's strange, Jeff thought. *That man's been here every day since we began this job.* Jeff threw some broken glass into the wheelbarrow.

Jeff and four friends had started a business during this school vacation. It was called Clean-Up Crew, Inc. The crew was cleaning a city block. Several buildings there had burned down six years ago.

Jeff wheeled his loaded wheelbarrow toward a huge trash bin. On his way, he passed Nan. She was working in the farthest corner of the block. "Hey, Nan," Jeff said, "what do you think about our audience?" He nodded his head toward the man who watched them.

"He gives me the creeps!" Nan said. "He scares Jill and Kim, too."

"He seems to watch you more than anyone," Jeff replied.

Nan shivered. "I don't look that pretty all covered with dirt," she said. "And neither does this pile of trash. So I can't figure out what he's looking at." She loaded some charred wood onto her wheelbarrow. "I wish my work area weren't so far from everyone else's."

*"Hey, Nan," Jeff said, "what do you think
of our audience?"*

"Maybe he'll be gone tomorrow," Jeff answered. "Let's stop for today. It's five o'clock. We've worked hard."

Nan and the rest of the crew brought their equipment to the waiting truck. Then they left for home.

The next morning, the chief of the fire department was waiting for them at the lot. "Who's in charge here?" he asked as they got off the truck.

"I am," Jeff responded.

"Well, I'd like to talk with you, then," the fire chief said.

The rest of the crew went off to work. They were very puzzled. Soon Jeff called everyone together. "Someone set a fire here last night," he told them.

"Why would someone set a fire *here*?" Jill asked.

"I don't know," Jeff replied. "It doesn't look as if there's anything but trash to burn, does it?"

"There *isn't* anything but trash," Bob answered. "I know. I've been digging through it for three days. Believe me, it's trash!"

The crew laughed nervously.

"It was your work area where the fire was set, Nan," Jeff said.

"I didn't set it!" Nan exclaimed.

"Of course you didn't," Jeff said. "The fire chief thinks someone may be trying to scare us away. He wants us to be on the lookout for anything strange."

"What about that man who keeps watching Nan?" Bob asked.

"Don't talk about him!" Nan exclaimed. "You're going to really frighten me, way off in my far corner."

"You'll be all right," Jeff said. "Now let's get to work."

They all headed back to their work

stations on the block. Soon, they were pushing filled wheelbarrows to the trash bin.

Nan made four trips to the bin that morning. "I'm getting closer to the bottom of that pile," she said to Kim as she walked by.

"Yes, and that guy is getting closer to you," Kim answered.

Nan started to turn in his direction.

"Don't look now!" Kim said. She grabbed Nan's arm. "There's something strange about this. I think he's afraid you're going to uncover something."

"Well, he can have whatever I uncover," Nan said angrily. "He can have every bit of trash!"

Nan went back to her work area on the far corner of the block. Soon she was busy trying to free some wire fence from the ground. She pulled at it, but it was partly buried in the dirt. She started to dig. She pulled at the fence and dug deeper. It was still stuck. She dug some more.

Suddenly, Nan stood very still. She was looking into the hole she had dug. Her face was completely white.

"Oh, no!" she cried. She knelt down and reached into the hole. The strange man moved toward her. Nan saw him. She jumped to her feet. She was holding a dirt-covered skull.

Nan started to run. The man ran after her. Jeff saw Nan dash across the street. She was heading for the alley. She knew that it was the fastest way to the police station.

Jeff shouted to the rest of the crew. Then he dashed across the street. Bob had been watching, too. He was already sprinting around the block. He hoped to

*Nan started to run. The man started
to run after her.*

cut the man off at the other end of the alley.

As she ran, Nan could hear the man gaining on her. She looked back over her shoulder. The man held a knife. She gripped the skull tighter and ran as fast as she could.

I should have run toward the rest of the crew for help, Nan thought. *But I didn't think he'd be able to keep up with me. Now I'm all alone.* Nan could feel her heart pounding. She knew it wasn't just because she was running.

I've got to make it out of this alley, she thought. *Maybe someone on the street will help me.* She put on a burst of speed.

Just as she left the alley, she saw Bob racing around the corner toward her. She turned again to look at the man. She saw Jeff and Jill coming up behind him.

She kept running.

When the man ran out of the alley, Bob was there. Bob tackled him, slamming him to the ground. In a few seconds, Jill and Jeff caught up. Jeff helped Bob pin the man down. Jill grabbed his knife.

Nan ran back when she heard the struggle. She was angry at the man for scaring her. "Why were you chasing me like that?" she yelled at him. "What do you know about this?" She pushed the skull at him.

"You nosy kids!" he shouted. "Why did you have to go digging around there? It was none of your business!"

Just then, a police car came speeding around the corner. It screeched to a halt right beside the man on the ground. A police officer jumped out.

Nan held up the skull. She started to

explain what had happened.

"I know," the officer interrupted. "Kim sent me after you."

He put handcuffs on the man. "We ran a check on this guy," the officer said. "We got suspicious after the fire the other day. I was just coming to pick him up for questioning.

"Six years ago," the policeman continued, "this man was suspected of having murdered three people. We had to let him go," he said. "We could never find the bodies."

Nan almost dropped the skull. "Now you know where the bodies are," she gasped.

"Now we know," he said. "Thanks to you. He buried the bodies. Then he burned down the buildings to hide them even more."

The officer pulled the man to his feet.

He read him his rights. Then he locked him in the squad car.

"I'll be back to dig up the other bodies," the officer said. He got in the car and drove away.

Everyone breathed a sigh of relief.

"You saved my life," Nan told her friends.

"We couldn't let anything happen to you. You're the hardest worker on the crew," Jeff joked. He put his arm around Nan. Then they all walked back to work.

That Clown on Roller Skates

Meg walked stiffly home from roller-skating practice. *Being a clown hurts,* she thought. Meg was a good roller skater. She had the lead in this year's show at school. She would star as a clown who couldn't skate. That meant she had to fall down a lot.

Meg carried her skates over her shoulder. *Am I sore!* she thought. She had been practicing a special fall. It was supposed to be like a sneeze that builds up and up — and then surprises everyone by being just a little "kerchoo."

I hope I don't have to fall much more, Meg thought. *I'm all black and blue.*

She walked down Main Street past all the busy stores. *I'm glad I can look in the windows,* she said to herself. *I'm too sore to walk fast.*

She headed down Maple Avenue. *It's quieter here,* she thought. *These shops are too expensive to draw large crowds.*

Meg walked along slowly. She was half-looking in the store windows and half-thinking about her clown act.

There's a pretty cat, she noticed. She watched a gray cat jump down from a window ledge. It peeked around the

*The cat peeked around the partly open door
of the Golden Antique Shop.*

partly open door of the Golden Antique Shop. As Meg limped along, the cat disappeared inside the store.

Meg read the sign in the window of the Golden Antique Shop as she walked by. "Shop closed for renovations. Will reopen September 5."

We've only got three practices left before September 5, Meg thought. *Then it will be opening night. I'm nervous already.* She walked down Maple Avenue, then turned onto Oak Street.

Cats are so graceful, Meg thought. *I wonder what they'd look like on roller skates.* She grinned as she pictured a cat with a skate on each foot.

"A cat," Meg said out loud. She stopped walking. Something felt strange to her. She couldn't tell what, though. She walked on a little bit farther. Then she stopped again.

The sign in the Golden Antique Shop window said the shop was closed, she realized. *But the cat walked in an open door. That's strange.*

Meg closed her eyes. She pictured the cat walking in the door. Then, she pictured the scene outside the shop. She remembered an unpleasant-looking man. He was standing near the back door of a red van. Meg hadn't looked at him for long. He looked too mean. But she could remember him clearly. He was angrily watching the cat go in the open door of the shop.

I bet he was robbing that shop. Maybe I should call the police. Meg looked around for a phone. *But what if the police came, and nothing was wrong? They'd think I was a real clown then!*

She sat on some steps to think. *I should go back there myself,* she decided.

But what if that man thinks I'm snoop-ing around?

I know! Meg thought in an instant. She quickly laced on her roller skates. Then she raced off like a speed skater.

When she got to the corner of Maple Avenue, Meg stopped. From then on, anyone looking at her would have thought she didn't know how to skate at all. She looked very awkward. She headed down Maple Avenue, hanging on to parking meters and trees.

Meg saw the red van ahead. It was still parked in front of the Golden An-tique Shop. The mean-looking man was there, too. He was putting something into the back of the van.

Meg didn't think about being sore now. She just wanted an excuse to watch what was happening. She fell down on the sidewalk with a grunt. The man looked around. He saw Meg sprawled on the sidewalk. But he must not have thought she was too much to worry about. He turned and walked into the Golden Antique Shop. And he left the door partly open.

Meg got up slowly. She skated closer to the shop. The man came out carrying a beautifully carved wooden clock. Meg started to flap her arms. She made one foot slide out in front as if she were going to fall.

The man glared at her as she got closer. He kept walking toward the van, though. Meg flapped her arms again as if she were trying not to fall. When she was even with the shop door, she leaned forward. She looked in through the slightly open door. She could see only a little bit inside, but she did see someone lying on the floor.

Meg gasped. The man turned quickly to look at her. She gasped again to make it sound as if she were just afraid of falling. The man kept staring at her.

"Hey, you! Get away from there," he shouted.

"I can't help it!" Meg cried. "I don't know how to skate." She began her clown fall. Her arms went in all directions. One leg kicked up. She slid sideways and bumped the door open the rest of the way with her foot.

There, lying on the floor by the counter, was a woman. There was blood on her forehead. She wasn't moving.

The man ran toward Meg. In a split second, she recovered from her fall. Before he could grab her, she was speeding off down the street.

When he realized he had been tricked, the man ran swiftly back toward the

*"I can't help it!" Meg cried. "I don't know
how to skate!"*

van. Meanwhile Meg skated to Main Street to find help.

Soon, she and two police officers were racing back up to Maple Avenue. Meg led them to the shop. The red van was gone. Most of the antiques were gone, too. But the woman on the floor was just coming around.

She told them that a man had hit her on the head. She could describe him a little. Then Meg gave a detailed description of the man and the van.

In three hours, the van was found. It still had all the antiques in it. An hour later, the man was caught.

He blamed his capture on "that clown on roller skates."

Meg was glad to take the blame.

Critter's Quite a Retriever!

Critter barked and ran around the yard. He would have cheered if he hadn't been a dog. His master, Danny, was playing catch with Mark, the little boy next door. Critter loved it. Mark was only three, so he missed the ball a lot. That meant Critter could "retrieve" it and run. Then Danny and Mark would have to chase him to get the ball back.

"I'm tired, Critter," Danny said finally, stretching out on the grass. Critter ran to the fence at the edge of the woods. He was carrying the ball. When Danny didn't chase him, Critter dropped the ball and barked.

"I don't feel like playing anymore, Critter," Danny said. "I've got baseball practice in a few minutes. I want to rest before I go."

Danny talked to Critter a lot. Critter was a smart dog. He always seemed to understand what Danny said to him. He didn't always behave, but Danny loved him anyway.

Critter left the ball by the fence and disappeared around the side of the house. Danny lay on the grass and watched Mark explore. In a few minutes, Critter came racing back. He was carrying a bicycle pump.

"Bad dog, Critter!" Danny yelled. Critter put the pump down in front of Danny. When he wanted to play, Critter "retrieved" anything that he could find.

"I'll have to find out where you got that later on. I've got to go to practice now." Danny tied Critter in the back yard. He brought Mark home to his mother and went to practice.

When Danny got home that afternoon, the neighborhood was all upset. Mark had disappeared.

Mark's mother was crying. She and her neighbors had searched all the yards and fields nearby. The police were searching now, too.

"I'll help," Danny said to his mother. "Where should I look?"

75

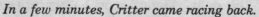

In a few minutes, Critter came racing back.

"It seems as if we've looked everywhere," she answered. "But you can look around the yards again. We might have missed him if he was unconscious."

"Did you check the woods?" Danny asked.

"There are wolves in there," she answered, shuddering. "Besides, the fence is too high for a little child to get over."

"O.K.," Danny answered. "I'll look in the yards again." He searched until dark, but had no luck.

When he got back to his own yard, Danny sat on the back porch to think. He could hear people calling Mark's name. He could also hear a wolf howling far away in the woods. *At least Mark's not in there,* Danny thought.

Critter was pulling at his chain. "Is the wolf scaring you, Critter?" Danny asked. He untied Critter so the dog could sit near him. But Critter ran over to the fence, sniffing all around. Then he started barking.

"Be quiet, Critter. You cause enough trouble in this neighborhood without making so much noise." Critter kept barking.

Danny walked toward Critter. All of a sudden, Critter disappeared behind a little bush. He reappeared on the other side of the fence.

Danny looked behind the bush. Some animal had dug a hole there under the fence. Suddenly, Danny remembered his mother's words, "The fence is too high for a little child to get over."

"But he could get *under* it, couldn't he?" Danny said aloud.

Critter started to bark again.

"Is Mark in the woods?" Danny asked the dog.

Critter barked and started to run into the woods.

"Wait," Danny said, hesitating. He thought about the wolves. Then he thought about Mark. He got his flashlight and baseball bat.

Danny squeezed his tall frame under the fence. He followed Critter into the dark woods. "Find Mark," Danny said to the dog.

Critter ran off through the woods, his nose to the ground. Danny tried to keep his flashlight shining on the dog. It was very hard to see in the woods, and Danny stumbled as he ran.

He called Mark's name. The wolf howled again. *That sounds too close,* Danny thought. He gripped the baseball bat tighter in his hands. *I hope that wolf is nowhere near Mark—if Mark is even here.*

Suddenly, Critter stood still. He pricked up his ears and tilted his head. Then he started to bark. He ran faster. Danny hurried to keep up with him, but soon Critter was out of sight.

Danny shone the flashlight back and forth, trying to find Critter with his light. The woods were very dark. Danny could see only unfamiliar shapes and shadows.

He must have taken off after that wolf, Danny thought when Critter didn't come back. Danny sat down on a log. *Now* I'm *lost,* he thought. He shut off the flashlight to save the batteries. Then he heard rustling sounds. He gripped the baseball bat tightly. There were more sounds.

Danny didn't know whether to call for Critter again or not. He didn't know whether to turn on the flashlight or not.

What if there's a wolf right near me? he thought nervously.

Then he heard a crying noise and more rustling. *That doesn't sound like a wolf*, he thought. He switched on the flashlight.

In the path of the light, Critter was pulling Mark by the shirt. Mark was covered with dirt and scratches. His clothes were torn.

"Mark!" Danny cried out. He ran to pick up the little boy.

"Good dog, Critter! You found Mark." Critter looked very pleased with himself.

"I went for a walk," Mark said.

"That was some walk!" Danny answered.

"I want my mommy," Mark said. Tears were streaking down his face.

"Your mommy wants you, too," Danny

"I want my mommy," Mark said.

answered. "We'll go home now." Then, for a moment, Danny was worried. *I hope Critter can get us out of here*, he thought.

"Let's go home, Critter," Danny said aloud.

Critter barked and started off through the woods. He ran on ahead and then waited. Danny hurried after him. They walked for a long time. Finally, Danny could see lights through the trees. *We're home,* he thought in relief. Critter started to bark, then he slipped through the hole under the fence.

Neighbors were still standing in their yards. "Mark's safe!" Danny shouted from the edge of the woods.

Everyone cheered and rushed to the fence. Danny passed Mark to his mother under the fence and then crawled under himself.

"Oh, thank you, Danny," she cried. "Thank you for finding Mark!"

"Critter found him," Danny said proudly. "He found him and brought him back to me."

"Critter's quite a retriever!" Mark's mother said happily.

"I think Critter 'retrieved' my bicycle pump today," another neighbor said. "But I won't be mad at him ever again. Not after this!"

"Or, at least, not until he 'retrieves' something else," Danny replied.

That Was Some Trout You Caught!

"There's no sign of it here." Sergeant Scott spoke into his walkie-talkie. His eyes searched the river. He was looking for a bottle of deadly poison.

"I'm going downstream. Over and out." Sergeant Scott waded through the water.

We've got to find that poison, Scott thought. *It would kill anyone who opens it — or breaks it.*

Another soldier was searching upstream from Sergeant Scott. The men had been transporting the poison to the Pittsfield Army Base. Their jeep had a blowout on the Deerfield River Bridge. The jeep had crashed, and both men were thrown free. Neither one was badly hurt, but the bottle of poison was lost in the river.

Half a mile downstream from the bridge, Timmy O'Brien was fishing. A few small fish had taken his bait, but he hadn't hooked anything big. *I'd love to have some trout for breakfast tomorrow morning,* he thought.

Timmy cast his line out into the river. He had gotten a fishing pole for his sixteenth birthday. Of all his possessions, this was his favorite. Every day since then, he had come to the river to fish. Soon he'd be back in school. He wanted to catch a big trout before then.

Timmy reeled in his line and checked his bait. Then he cast again. Almost as soon as his line sank in the river, Timmy could tell he had caught something. *Let this be a big one,* he thought.

Then, out of the corner of his eye, he saw something move. He looked up and spotted a soldier across the river. The soldier was staring into the water.

I wonder what he's doing here, Timmy thought. But the pressure on his line brought Timmy back to his fishing. The pull of the current was strong. *This is going to be a tough one,* he thought. He started to reel his catch in slowly.

Just then, he saw the soldier run into the river. The walkie-talkie was at his

*Timmy looked up and spotted a soldier
across the river.*

mouth. He was pointing at the middle of the river. Timmy was so startled that he almost dropped his pole.

"Hang on to that pole!" the soldier yelled to Timmy. Then he shouted into the walkie-talkie. "I can see it! A boy has it on his fishing line!"

The soldier struggled against the current, pushing his way out into the river. "I'm Sergeant Scott," he shouted to Timmy. "I need your help."

"What's going on?" Timmy asked.

"You've got something on your line," Sergeant Scott called out.

"I know," Timmy said. "I think it's a big one, too."

"It's not a fish," Scott answered.

"What is it?" Timmy asked. "An old shoe?"

"Can you keep your head in an emergency?" the soldier asked. He couldn't go any farther out into the river without getting the walkie-talkie wet.

"I don't know," Timmy answered. "I was never in one before."

"Well, you're in one now. And you can save a lot of lives if you can stay cool."

"I'll try," Timmy said. He started to reel in his line.

"Wait!" Sergeant Scott yelled. "You've got a bottle of poison on your line. You've got to land it carefully."

"Poison!" Timmy exclaimed. "I don't want to land any poison!" He felt like dropping his pole and running home.

"That poison was lost in a crash. We've been searching for it for hours," Sergeant Scott said. "If someone opens it or if it breaks, many people will die. If you can land it safely, you'll be a hero."

"I don't want to be a hero," Timmy said. "I'll try to land it, though."

"Don't let it bump against any rocks," the soldier said.

"The current is strong," Timmy replied. "What if I can't keep it away from the rocks?" His heart was pounding.

"I'm not sure," Sergeant Scott said. "It might break, and it might not. If it does, get away from here fast."

"What about you?" Timmy asked, looking at the man standing up to his shoulders in the river.

"It will be too late for me," the soldier answered. "But you can land it safely. Pretend it's a big trout." He smiled at Timmy. "Bring it in."

Timmy looked carefully into the water. He started to reel in his line. Soon he, too, could see the white bottle through the green river water.

"If I go out into the river past these rocks, I'll have a better chance to get it,"

Timmy told the soldier.

"But then you'll have no chance if it breaks," the soldier answered quietly. "Then if it breaks, you'll die."

"If I don't and it breaks, a lot of other people will die, won't they?" Timmy asked.

"Yes," Sergeant Scott replied.

Timmy didn't say anything more. He walked into the river. He stepped carefully over the rocks. Soon, he was up to his waist in the water.

"It looks free from this angle," Timmy said.

"It looks O.K. from this side, too," the soldier replied.

"I'm bringing it in then," Timmy said. He reeled his line in, bringing the bottle of poison closer and closer. Soon, it was right beside him in the water.

Timmy reached out and picked up the bottle. He tried to steady his hand so he could remove the hook from the plastic handle where it had gotten stuck. Then Timmy held the bottle up for the soldier to see.

"He's got it!" the soldier shouted into the walkie-talkie.

Timmy could hear a cheer come out of the walkie-talkie.

"Wait there with it," the soldier said to Timmy. "I'm going back to the bridge to cross over. Then I'll help you get past the rocks with it." The soldier turned and pushed back toward the shore.

Timmy stood in the water, holding the bottle with both hands. He had let go of his pole when he got the hook out of the poison bottle. Somehow the pole didn't seem so important anymore.

Soon, Sergeant Scott was shouting to Timmy, "I'm almost there!"

The sergeant put his walkie-talkie on

Timmy held the bottle up for the soldier to see.

the shore. He climbed over the rocks and hurried out to where Timmy was standing in the river.

"Let's get back to shore," Sergeant Scott said. The two of them moved carefully through the water. Scott helped to steady Timmy as they crossed the rocks. Finally, they were on land.

Timmy put the poison bottle down on the ground. "It's safe now," the soldier said.

Timmy felt his legs start to tremble. He sat down on the grass. Sergeant Scott sat beside him. He reached out to shake Timmy's hand.

"That was some trout you caught!" the soldier said.

"It was a tough one," Timmy answered. "I lost my pole trying to land it."

"The President will get you a new one," Sergeant Scott said.

"The President?" Timmy said in amazement.

"Yes," Sergeant Scott answered. "I'm sure the President will have a special fishing rod for a hero like you."

"Well, I ought to be able to catch a trout with a fishing pole from the President," Timmy said.

Then he lay back in the grass. He looked up at the sky and smiled.